Pet Your Pet

Written by Dana Meachen Rau
Illustrated by Jeffrey Scherer

Reading Advisers:

Gail Saunders-Smith, Ph.D., Reading Specialist

Dr. Linda D. Labbo, Department of Reading Education,
College of Education, The University of Georgia

LEVEL B

A COMPASS POINT
EARLY READER

For Honey, Doolittle, and Bramble

A Note to Parents

As you share this book with your child, you are showing your new reader what reading looks like and sounds like. You can read to your child any-where—in a special area in your home, at the library, on the bus, or in the car. Your child will associate reading with the pleasure of being with you.

This book will introduce your young reader to many of the basic con-cepts, skills, and vocabulary necessary for successful reading. Talk through the details in each picture before you read. Then read the book to your child. As you read, point to each word, stopping to talk about what the words mean and the pictures show. Your child will begin to link the sounds of the letters with the look of the words that you and he or she read.

After your child is familiar with the story, let him or her read the story alone. Be careful to let the young reader make mistakes and correct them on his or her own. Be sure to praise the young reader's abilities. And, above all, have fun.

Gail Saunders-Smith, Ph.D.
Reading Specialist

Consulting editor: Rebecca McEwen

Compass Point Books
3722 West 50th Street, #115
Minneapolis, MN 55410

Visit Compass Point Books on the Internet at *www.compasspointbooks.com* or e-mail your request to *custserv@compasspointbooks.com*

Library of Congress Cataloging-in-Publication Data
Rau, Dana Meachen.
   Pet your pet / written by Dana Meachen Rau ; illustrated by Jeffrey Scherer.
     p. cm. — (Compass Point early reader)
   "Level B."
   Summary: Presents rhyming suggestions for a number of ways to show affection to a variety of pets.
   ISBN 0-7565-0175-X (hardcover)
   [1. Pets—Fiction. 2. Stories in rhyme.] I. Scherer, Jeffrey, ill. II. Title. III. Series.
   PZ8.3.R232 Pe 2002
   [E]—dc21   2001004726

Pet your pet on its fur.

That is how you make her purr.

Pet your pet on its shell.

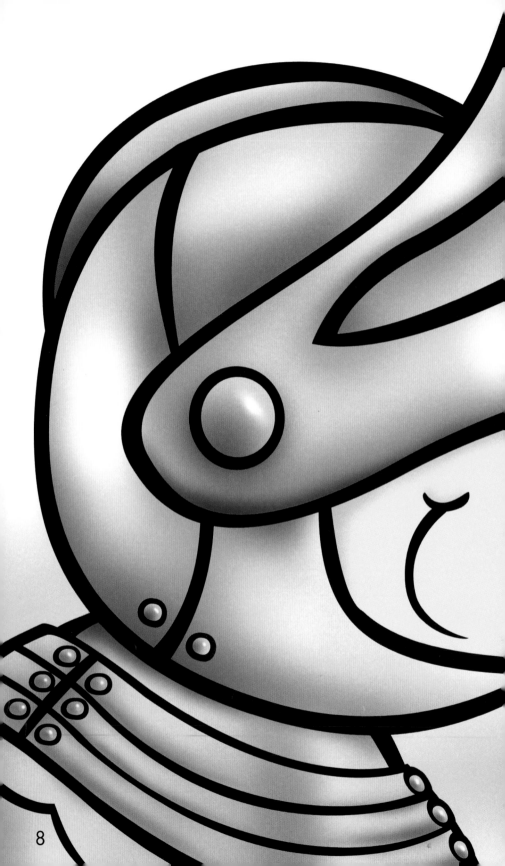

He will like it, you can tell.

Pet your pet up on top.

She'll wag her tail
until you stop.

Pet your pet on its side.

Then hop on up
and take a ride.

Pet your pet on its chin.

He'll be so happy,
he just might grin.

Pet your pet
on its chest.

He will say he loves you best.

Pet your pet ten times a day.

He'll love you back
in his own way.

29

More Fun with Pets!

Does your family have a pet? Pets are a great way to teach children responsibility. Pets need to be taken care of, because just like kids, they need to eat, sleep, exercise, and sometimes even take a bath. But most importantly, pets give kids the opportunity to show affection. Let your children know that petting a pet every day really does make the pet, and

them, feel good.
If your
child doesn't
have a pet,
or can't
because of
allergies, try this
activity. Take out
some paper
and crayons or
markers and make
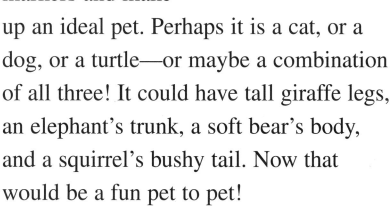
up an ideal pet. Perhaps it is a cat, or a
dog, or a turtle—or maybe a combination
of all three! It could have tall giraffe legs,
an elephant's trunk, a soft bear's body,
and a squirrel's bushy tail. Now that
would be a fun pet to pet!

Word List

(In this book: 54 words)

a	in	side
and	is	so
back	it	stop
be	its	tail
best	just	take
can	like	tell
chest	love	ten
chin	loves	that
day	make	then
fur	might	times
grin	on	top
happy	own	until
he	pet	up
he'll	purr	wag
her	ride	way
his	say	will
hop	she'll	you
how	shell	your

About the Author

Dana Rau grew up with a cat named Honey. She was tan and white and loved curling up to sleep on top of Dana' homework. Today, Dana lives with her husband, Chris, and children, Charlie and Allison, in Farmington, Connecticut, where she writes a lot of children's books. They don't have a pet yet, but Charlie thinks if they do get one, it should be a gorilla or an ostrich.

About the Illustrator

Jeffrey Scherer is a children's book illustrator and graphi artist in Albany, New York. He was once the proud owne of thirteen zebra finches. His favorite was a white one called Blanco. These days, Jeffrey and his wife, Winnie, are busy raising two daughters, Samantha and Stephanie But he would consider a Rhode Island red hen for a pet because they eat bugs and lay fresh eggs. This is his seventh children's book.